The Seaside Puppy

The Seaside Puppy

by Holly Webb

Illustrated by Sophy Williams

tiger tales

tiger tales

5 River Road, Suite 128, Wilton, CT 06897
Published in the United States 2019
Originally published in Great Britain 2016
by the Little Tiger Group
Text copyright © 2016, 2019 Holly Webb
Illustrations copyright © 2016, 2019 Sophy Williams
ISBN-13: 978-1-68010-437-0
ISBN-10: 1-68010-437-3
Printed in China
STP/1800/0327/1219
All rights reserved
10 9 8 7 6 5 4 3 2

For more insight and activities, visit us at www.tigertalesbooks.com

Contents

For Eva

Chapter One
Summer Vacation!

"Are you going on vacation?" Max asked Jessie, whacking at a thistle bush with a stick as they walked home from school along the road. "We're going to Florida on Saturday."

"Yes, we are, but not until the end of August, just before we go back to school," Jessie said. "We're going to Colorado for a week to stay with my grandma."

"We can't," Laura said, a little sadly. Almost everybody in her class seemed to be going somewhere amazing, but she was staying at home all summer. She gave a tiny sigh and peered over the bushes to catch a glimpse of the ocean. It was really blue, and the sun was making the ripples glitter. Laura knew they were lucky to live in such a beautiful place, but it would have been nice to go on vacation somewhere different!

"Mom's working," Laura went on. "Summer is the busiest time of year for her. All the cottages are booked up for the entire 10 weeks. She says she's going to be run off her feet."

Jessie nodded. "It's okay. I'll be

around until the end of August. We can go to the beach. Mom has signed me up for some bodyboarding lessons for the first couple weeks. I want to get a lot of practice in."

Max snorted. "Yeah, you *need* the practice."

Jessie blew a cloud of dandelion seeds at him so they caught in his blond hair, coating it in white fluff. It made him look about 60 years older all of a sudden.

"Ugh, get them off me! Yuck." Max flailed at his hair, annoyed. "They're all itchy."

9

"Serves you right," Laura pointed out. "Just because you've been surfing since you could stand up, doesn't mean you have to be critical of Jessie. She's only lived here a year!" She smiled gratefully at Jessie, really glad that someone was going to be around for most of the summer.

Many of their friends lived a long way from Sandyhill and took the school bus, so it wasn't that easy to meet up with them during vacations. Mom had promised Laura that they'd try to fit in some time to go to the beach together, but Laura knew how busy she would be. Laura didn't like seeing her so tired. Managing the cottages meant that Mom was on duty 24 hours a day, really, in case any of the guests had a problem.

Laura helped out as much as she could, although mostly she sat and did her homework while Mom was cleaning the cottages. But this vacation, now that Laura was almost 10, they'd agreed that she was old enough to stay at home while Mom was out. The vacation cottages and the little cottage where she and Mom lived had all been converted from old farm buildings, so Mom would never be that far away. Since the beginning of the school year, she'd let Laura walk to and from school with Max and Jessie. Laura was even allowed to go to the beach for a little bit by herself or with friends. She wasn't allowed to swim on her own, though. Mom had made her promise.

The best thing was that during the

last few weeks, Mom had let her go into town by herself to do some of the shopping. Laura had been begging for a while—after all, everyone in the stores knew her, she'd told Mom. It made a big difference, with Mom not having to do all the shopping as well as everything else. Laura loved seeing her come home, look in the fridge, and say how nice it was to have everything done.

They were coming into town now, and Jessie and Max waved good-bye as they headed down their street. Laura had to go on a little farther—Sandyhill Farm, where she lived, was just on the other side of town.

Laura sped up as she saw Mrs. Eccles out for a walk with her Jack Russell, Toby. Mrs. Eccles had been Laura's teacher in kindergarten. She'd retired a couple of years ago and got Toby to keep her company.

"Hello, Laura! It's the last day of school, isn't it?" Mrs. Eccles called. "Are you excited about vacation?"

Laura crouched down to rub Toby's ears. He was such a sweet dog, even though Mrs. Eccles said he was really naughty and a terrible thief.

"Don't give that little rascal too much attention," she said to Laura. "He ate my breakfast this morning. An entire piece of toast! I don't think he even chewed it—it just went straight down his throat. Little monster, aren't you?" she told Toby lovingly, and he sat there beating his tail hard against the pavement. He loved being petted, and Laura was one of his favorite people.

"Oh, you silly dog," Laura muttered, scratching under his chin. "You'll get too big!"

"Luckily, he goes three times as far as I do whenever we're out for a walk, with all the dashing around, sniffing, and chasing butterflies," Mrs. Eccles said. "We're going all the way to the lighthouse this afternoon. He can work off that toast! See you soon, Laura. Have a wonderful first day of summer vacation!"

Laura waved as Mrs. Eccles and Toby turned down the side street that led to the cliff path. A long walk all the way to the lighthouse with handsome Toby.... She watched enviously as they disappeared around the corner. Walks were so much more fun with a dog. She'd seen Toby chasing sticks and balls, jumping in and out of the ocean, and barking at the waves. Maybe Mrs. Eccles would let her come along with them at some point over vacation! Laura nodded to herself. She'd ask Mrs. Eccles the next time she saw them.

Henry padded uncertainly through the house, sniffing at the furniture. He didn't understand what was happening. He felt dizzy and a little sick from being in the car for so long. And when they'd gotten out, they weren't back home. They were somewhere else.

But at least Annie was here. She was rushing around with the others, up and down the stairs, throwing doors open. They kept shouting. One of the boys had tripped over Henry and then stepped on his tail—so now the puppy was keeping out of the way. *Maybe this is my new home*, he thought worriedly, sitting down under the kitchen table in a forest of chair legs.

"Hey, Henry!" Annie crouched down to pat him. "Are you all right? Did you find your basket? Here, look."

Henry followed her over to the corner of the kitchen and sniffed obediently at his basket.

Fortunately, *that* was the same. Annie

17

put down a bowl of water, which he drank eagerly. But when he looked up, she'd disappeared again, and his ears drooped. He climbed into the basket, slumped down with his muzzle sticking out over the edge, and waited.

He wasn't really sure what he was waiting for. A walk? For Annie to come back and pick him up? He lay there, listening, his ears flicking. Every so often, he thumped his tail on his cushioned basket when he heard someone come past. But no one stopped to pet him. Eventually, Henry drifted off to sleep.

Chapter Two
Meeting Henry

"I'm worried about that big group in the old farmhouse." Laura's mom sighed. "I just went over to check on how they're settling in. The entire house is a mess already, and they just got here! Bags and clothes all over the place. I don't think any of them is older than 18. My guess is that they're on vacation together because they just finished their exams."

"Are they staying long?" Laura asked, pouring milk over her cereal. She was still in her pajamas, looking forward to a lazy breakfast with no need to rush off to school.

"Two weeks!" Mom rolled her eyes. "I guess it means less hassle with not having to change over the farmhouse for another family after a week, but I wish they were a little more responsible." She sighed again, and then smiled at Laura. "They've brought a very cute little dog with them, though. It's a spaniel, I think. I'm sure you'd know, Laura."

Laura sat up straighter and peered out the kitchen window, wondering if she might see the little dog.

The old farmhouse was the biggest of the vacation homes, and it was just across the pretty paved yard from Laura and her mom's cottage. The farmhouse was right next to the road that led down to the beach, and it had amazing views of the ocean. It was always booked solid in during the summer. But right now, the house looked quiet. All the curtains were still closed, and there was certainly no sign of a dog.

Mom laughed. "Are you going to spend the day staring out the window to see if they go for a walk?"

"No...," Laura said, going back to her cereal. But secretly she was thinking that it wouldn't be all that difficult to accidentally-on-purpose run into the dog and his or her owner.

Later that afternoon, Laura was shooting a ball at the basketball hoop in the courtyard when she heard a door closing behind her and a boy's loud voice.

"Come on, Henry! Let's go!"

Laura looked around, wondering who Henry was, and feeling a little sorry for him. Then she gave a delighted gasp.

A beautiful King Charles spaniel was sniffing at the huge flowerpots on either side of the farmhouse door. He was only a puppy, Laura guessed—he was really little. He bounced around on short legs, yipping excitedly and flapping his fluffy ears. Mom had been right about his breed. Laura had seen King Charles spaniels before, but never a tiny puppy like this one. She giggled as she saw his big orange eyebrows. They gave his face such a sweet, grumpy look.

"Oh, he's beautiful. How old is he?" Laura asked, hurrying over to the teenage boy who was pulling at the puppy's leash. She was sure that someone who was walking such a handsome dog would be happy to talk about him. Who wouldn't want to show off a puppy like that?

"What?" the boy said, staring at her. His voice didn't sound very friendly, and Laura's cheeks turned pink.

"I-I just wondered how old he was," she stuttered. "He looks very small."

"No idea. Come on, Henry, stop messing around."

The boy tugged at the puppy's leash and finally managed to drag him away from the flowerpots and out into the yard.

The puppy pulled back against his collar, whining a little, and Laura bit her lip. She wanted to tell the boy not to yank at his neck like that—that he was hurting him. But she wasn't quite brave enough. The puppy, Henry, belonged to this boy, or at least to one of his friends. She didn't have any right to tell him off.

Then the puppy seemed to catch the scent of the ocean. He sniffed deeply and his ears twitched, and he followed the boy happily around the corner of the farmhouse, toward the path that led down to the beach. Laura watched them go, then slowly walked back to her cottage.

Henry sat up and yawned, then peered over the edge of his basket. It was still much too large for him, but his toys helped to fill up the rest of the space.

He stared over at the kitchen door and heaved a great sigh. Then he nosed thoughtfully at his squishy ball, pushing it against the side of the basket. It let out a faint squeak and he batted at it with his paw—but it wasn't as much fun without someone to throw it for him.

Henry gazed over at the door again. Where were they? He was sure that he'd been asleep for a long time. And he needed to go out.... He'd had a short walk earlier with one of the boys, just down the road a little way. There hadn't been time for much exploring, but at least he'd had the chance to go pee. Now he definitely needed to go again. He knew he shouldn't pee in the house—and there wasn't even any newspaper down. But he just couldn't wait any longer.

Henry climbed out of his basket, looking around uncertainly. Then he made a puddle and hurried away from it guiltily.

He was starting to feel hungry, too. It was such a long time since breakfast. He was used to three meals a day, and now that he thought about it, he felt miserably empty. He went padding around the kitchen, sniffing for something to eat. He scratched at the door of the cupboard where he'd seen Annie put his bag of dog food, but it didn't open.

Slowly he wandered out of the kitchen and into the big living room. There were bags and clothes scattered around on the floor and over the couches, and he wondered if some of them might have food in them. One red bag smelled delicious. A sweet, rich smell—much nicer than his dog food. The bag was zipped shut, though, and no matter hard he scratched at the fabric, he couldn't get in.

Henry sat back and looked at it. He was hungrier than ever now. He felt as though he could just eat the entire bag.... He wagged his feathery tail briskly and crouched down by the side of the bag, baring his sharp little teeth. It only took a few minutes to chew through the side and pull out a package of cookies. The plastic caught in his teeth as he tore the package open, but

Henry didn't mind too much.

He gobbled up all of them, then stretched happily and flopped down on top of the soft red bag for a nap. All that biting at the tough fabric had worn him out.

Chapter Three
Henry in Trouble

Henry's ears twitched a little as he heard voices and footsteps, and then the door banging.

"Look at my bag!"

Henry woke up with a start. Someone was shouting. He could almost feel the noise, as if the air was shaking. With a tiny whimper, he pressed himself down into the soft fabric of his basket. Were they shouting at him?

"Ooo, that dog! He ruined it. Look, it's chewed to pieces!"

"Oh, Molly. I'm really sorry. Henry, you bad dog! Bad dog!"

Annie had crouched down next to the basket, and she said the words in a loud, angry voice—not at all like the voice she usually used.

Henry whimpered again. It was definitely him they were angry with. But why? Annie never spoke to him like that. He quivered his tail, just a little, to show he was sorry, but she didn't seem to notice.

He watched miserably as Annie stood up and turned to the other girl, looking at the bag he'd eaten the cookies from earlier that day. She pulled out the chewed-up scraps of the package and sighed. "I guess it's my fault. He was hungry—I should have given him something before we went out. I'll get you a new bag, Molly!"

Annie put her arm around Molly's shoulders and led her out into the yard. Henry watched them go, his ears drooping. Those cookies seemed like such a long time ago....

"I had a feeling that group of teenagers was going to be difficult," Laura's mom sighed as she put her phone away. "That was the lady who's staying next door to them. She said they were still out in the yard at midnight, shouting and playing music."

Laura looked at her in surprise. "I didn't hear anything."

Mom shook her head. "No, I didn't, either, but I guess if we were already asleep, we might not have. And the yard is behind the farmhouse, between it and the lady's cottage. So the noise probably traveled that way."

"I hope Henry wasn't scared by the noise," Laura said.

"Henry? Oh, the little dog. Is that his name?" Mom smiled. "I might have known you'd find that out."

"I saw one of the boys taking him for a walk," Laura explained. "He's so cute—he's really tiny. I don't think that boy liked him very much, though," she added, frowning as she remembered. "He just kept telling him to come on, and yanking at his leash."

"Oh, dear…. Maybe it wasn't his dog." The phone suddenly shrilled again, and Mom pulled it out of her pocket, looking at it anxiously. "Hello? Oh, hello. I see. No, that's not good. And you took him back? Well, thank you. Yes, of course, I'll have a word with them. Thanks so much."

She ended the call and rolled her eyes at Laura. "That was the family from the cottage on the other side of the farmhouse. They just found a little dog in their kitchen, eating their lunch!"

"What?" Laura blinked at her.

"They'd left their back door open, and he just walked in. They found him

35

standing on the kitchen table, eating a plate of sandwiches."

Laura giggled. It was pretty funny. But poor Henry! The man on the phone had sounded really annoyed. She'd heard him even from across the kitchen table, and she was worried he would have yelled at the puppy. Henry had probably gotten scared.

"I think I'd better go over to the cottage and make sure everything else is all right," Mom said. "They were kind enough to take Henry back to the farmhouse, but they weren't happy. And then I guess I'd better go and talk to his owner." She sighed. "You'll be all right here, won't you, Laura? Maybe when I get back we could play a game of ping pong." She gave Laura a hug. "I'm sorry, sweetheart. I was hoping we'd be able to spend some time together today, since we haven't really had a chance since school got out."

"It's okay," Laura said. "I might go for a walk along the clifftop. Max said there was going to be a lifeboat display this afternoon, with a rescue helicopter. I can go and watch from the path. Though knowing Max, he probably got the day wrong!"

Mom laughed. "Okay. I'll see you in a bit. Have fun!"

Laura grabbed her little backpack and slipped an apple in for a snack, along with a water bottle—it felt even hotter this afternoon. Then she let herself out the front door. Of course, taking the cliff path meant going right past the farmhouse….

She was worried about Henry. That boy walking him yesterday had sounded really grumpy. And now the little puppy had been running loose! Surely his owners hadn't just let him out, had they? Laura chewed her lip anxiously. Either Henry had been let out on purpose, or he'd slipped away and they hadn't even noticed that he was gone. She wasn't sure which was worse.

As Laura walked across the yard, one of the girls from the farmhouse came around the corner and smiled at her. She had very bright blue eyes and curly dark hair, and she looked really friendly.

Laura smiled back.

"You live here, don't you?" the older girl asked her. "You're so lucky! I can't imagine living somewhere so beautiful all year round."

"It is nice," Laura agreed. "Pretty cold and windy in the winter, though. Are you here because it's the end of your exams?"

"Mm-hmm. We're all friends from school. I'm Annie, by the way."

"I'm Laura," Laura told her, a little shyly.

"I saw the dog who's staying with you at the farmhouse yesterday. He's so sweet."

Annie rolled her eyes. "He's mine. He is sweet, but he's been really naughty since we got here. I guess it's just strange for him, being in a new place. He chewed up my friend Molly's purse—she was furious. And then this morning I didn't get around to taking him out before we went food shopping, and he got out. Poor Henry. It's a pain that we can't bring him to the beach with us. Logan took him out for a walk yesterday, but he's been stuck here at the house since. I think maybe he's bored."

"Oh, but you can take dogs on most of the beach," Laura explained. "Just not Gull Cove—that's the part closest to town."

"Oh, okay. That's the nice sandy part, though, isn't it?"

"Well, if...." Laura gulped nervously, then decided that the worst thing Annie could say to her was no. "If you think Henry needs some exercise while you're out, maybe I could take him for a walk along the beach here."

Annie stared at her. "Really?"

"Yeah. I love dogs, and I don't have one. I'd like to. Um, if you think that would be okay."

"Sure." Annie beamed at her. "That would be great. You can take him now, if you'd like. I'll go and get him."

"Oh!" Laura nodded eagerly. "Right now? Yes, please!"

Annie grinned at her and headed into the farmhouse while Laura waited in the yard. She was so excited she was actually hopping from foot to foot, she realized. Her cheeks turned pink, and she put both feet very firmly on the ground. Annie wouldn't want her to take Henry out if she thought Laura was being silly.

Laura knew she should go and tell her mom, but she pushed the thought to the back of her mind. Mom had gone to talk to the people at one of the cottages, so she couldn't ask right now. And Laura was pretty sure Mom wouldn't mind. After all, she'd said that Henry was really cute, hadn't she?

Then Annie came out with Henry, and all thoughts about asking Mom first went out of Laura's head entirely. He was just so handsome. He was peeking shyly around Annie's legs, looking up at Laura with his head to one side. A bright red collar and leash stood out against the black fur of his neck, and his white paws were spotlessly clean.

Laura crouched down and slowly put out one hand for Henry to sniff.

"You're sure it's all right for me to take him?" Laura said as the puppy eyed her cautiously.

"Of course." Annie put the leash into Laura's hand and patted Henry. "Be good, Henry-dog! Oh! I almost forgot." She darted back into the house. "You might need these. Poop bags." She made a face. "I know, it's a little disgusting…."

Laura shook her head. "No. I mean, it is, but it would be worse just leaving it for someone to step in. Thanks." She tucked the bags in her pocket and looked down at the puppy. "Going to come for a walk, Henry?" Then she giggled as Henry's tail began to sweep from side to side, faster and faster. He obviously knew what that word meant. She tugged gently on his leash and set off around the side of the farmhouse, down the path to the clifftop and the beach.

Henry followed, a little confused by this new person. But then he'd seen a lot of new people during the last few days. The house was full of strange, big, noisy people. Whenever he was settling down to sleep, or trying to climb on Annie's lap for a cuddle, someone would clomp by loudly, or fling himself down onto the couch.

He trotted after the girl, liking the low voice she was using to coax him along and the way she didn't pull at his leash.

The narrow path that led to the cliffs was a little overgrown, but it smelled amazing to a small dog. Henry stopped to plunge his nose among the clumps of grass, shaking his feathery ears in excitement. He snorted delightedly, sniffing among the weeds, and the girl laughed.

"Is that nice?" she asked. "What can you smell? Is it rabbits?"

Henry looked up at her, wagging his tail, and then licked her hand. The sun was warm on his fur, and the air was full of good smells. This girl wasn't hurrying him along like that boy, Logan, had the day before. She didn't seem to mind how long he spent investigating everything. He panted happily and headed on down the path.

Chapter Four
An Afternoon Adventure

Laura looked down at Henry thoughtfully. He was prancing along, although he did keep stopping to sniff at something every couple of feet, which slowed them down a little. Even though he was so bouncy, she wasn't sure how far he'd be able to walk. She knew King Charles spaniels could be energetic, but he was still little—and she didn't think that Annie had been taking him on long walks, either.

"We'd better not go too far," she said. "Let's walk down the path to the beach. This is Warren Cove. I bet you smelled all the rabbits up on the cliff, didn't you?"

Henry scurried down the path ahead of her, ears flapping in the breeze. As the scrubby grass turned to sand and pebbles, he stopped, lifting up each front paw, and then putting them down again, looking confused. This gritty stuff between his paws was new, his expression said quite clearly.

"Haven't you been on the beach at all?" Laura said, surprised. "Oh, of course— they thought you weren't allowed. It's sand. Don't you like it? Look, you can dig." She crouched down and dug a hole in the sand, right in front of Henry's nose. He gave a squeaky little yelp and plunged both forepaws in right away, scratching madly and sending sand flying all over the place.

Laura sat back, laughing and holding up her hand to shield her face. "I'm going to have to brush you before I give you back—you're covered!"

The puppy's long fur was clotted with golden sand, especially in the pretty feathery parts around his paws and chest.

"Unless you want to go for a swim, of course," Laura said, looking thoughtfully at the ocean. It was beautifully calm today—a still, glassy greenish-blue, with little creamy waves breaking onto the pebbles. "Come on, Henry. Let's go and take a look at the ocean." She jumped up, patting at her leg, and Henry trotted after her.

Henry slowed down as they got closer to the water and stared at it suspiciously.

"It's okay," Laura whispered, kicking off her flip-flops and crouching down next to him. "I know, it's funny, isn't it? It keeps going in and out."

Henry looked up at her and wagged his tail uncertainly. He didn't understand what the ocean was at all. But the girl didn't sound very worried by it. She didn't step back when it came hissing and foaming toward them.

Laura stayed crouching next to Henry. She hoped he would go into the water—she knew a lot of dogs loved swimming. It would wash some of the sand off, too. And she couldn't help imagining how handsome he'd look, paddling around in the ocean…. She didn't want to make him, though.

Henry took a step forward, and then barked in surprise as the water made a rush at him, sucking the sand out from beneath his paws. It was cold! He shook his paws, then barked again as the drops splashed and sparkled around him.

Laura giggled, and he looked up at her. "Do you like it?" she asked. She couldn't quite tell.

Henry stayed put, even though the next wave came right up to his tummy. He jumped and barked at the ripples and the yellowish foam.

Laura was just thinking how much fun it would be to come down with her bathing suit on one day, so she and Henry could play in the water, when a sudden loud roaring made her jump. She almost slipped, but then she clapped a hand over her mouth and laughed. "Oh! Oh, wow, a helicopter!"

It was flying around the curve of the cliffs that shaped the little bay and divided the two beaches. The tall cliffs had shielded Laura and Henry from the sound of the rotors until it came right into the bay.

"I guess it's on the way to that lifeboat display Max was talking about," Laura said.

The leash suddenly jerked in her hands, and Laura looked down in surprise. "Oh, Henry!"

The puppy was whining in fright, tugging frantically at the leash and backing away across the sand.

He hated the noise. He'd never heard anything so loud, and he could feel the ground shaking.

"Don't worry." Laura picked him up, hugging the tiny dog tightly. She could tell he was really scared—he was shivering in her arms. "It's okay. It's just a helicopter. It was noisy, though, wasn't it?" She continued talking softly to calm him down as the helicopter flew across the bay.

55

At last it disappeared around the other side of the cliffs. "It's gone now," she said gently. "Come on, sweetie. Do you want to paddle a little more?" She rubbed her hand over his silky ears, and he snuggled against her, burying his head in her T-shirt.

"Maybe we'd better just head home," Laura muttered, grabbing her flip-flops and wobbling as she tried to put them back on without letting go of Henry. "I don't know if that helicopter is going to come past again." She picked her way slowly across the stones toward the steps that led up from the other end of the beach.

Henry wriggled in her arms as he picked up the scent of a patch of half-dried seaweed. Laura thought it smelled disgusting, but she supposed it might be nice if you were a dog. She put him down so he could check it out. At least it was distracting him from the scary helicopter.

Finally Henry lost interest in the seaweed and went sniffing his way across the beach toward the path. He was still a little twitchy, Laura noticed. When he heard another dog barking from up on the cliffs, he jumped and pressed himself against her legs.

Laura kept talking to him as they walked up the cliff path—saying comforting things about how nice the hot sun was, and how she loved the sharp smell of the sage growing along the path. She could see he was listening to her. Of course, he didn't understand what she was saying, but Laura was sure that didn't matter.

They stopped at the top, and Laura let out a huge sigh. "That path is so steep!" She glanced down at Henry, who was panting, too. He flopped onto the ground, looking tired and hot.

"You need a drink," Laura said, sitting down beside him and opening up her backpack. She looked at her water bottle, wondering if Henry would let her dribble some water in his mouth. She wished she'd thought of bringing him a bowl. Henry was still panting, with fast, short little breaths. He sounded miserable.

"This will have to do," Laura told him, cupping one hand and pouring some water into it. She saw Henry's ears flicking as he heard the splashing sound, and he sat up eagerly. She held her hand under his nose, and at first he just looked at it, confused. Then he realized what she was doing and lapped eagerly at the water. It was gone in seconds.

"More?" Laura refilled her hand, giggling as Henry's soft pink tongue swept over her palm. "You really are thirsty."

Henry drank five handfuls of water, and then flopped down again. But this time he looked much happier. He was resting his chin on his paws as he watched the bees buzzing through the wildflowers by the path.

Laura sat rubbing his back, feeling the sun on her hair and pretending, just for a moment, that Henry was hers.

"I'd take you on a lot of walks," she whispered. "Of course, I'd always bring your water bowl. And I'd never let a helicopter come anywhere near you." She smiled to herself. As if she could stop a helicopter! But it was all just imagining, anyway. Henry was someone else's puppy.

"I guess we should get going," Laura sighed at last. "Come on, Henry. It isn't too far, I promise."

Henry heaved himself up and padded along the grassy path after Laura. He wasn't as bouncy as he had been when they'd set off, but he still looked like he was enjoying himself. When a butterfly fluttered over his nose, he yapped excitedly and tried to jump up at it. He didn't get anywhere near it, of course, and he watched grumpily as the butterfly whirled away.

Laura laughed. "You are a funny thing," she told him. "What would you do with a butterfly if you caught it, anyway?"

They were almost home when a couple of seagulls came diving by. Huge white herring gulls with wide, gray wings. They swooped over Laura and Henry, shrieking, and Henry squealed in fright. He was still nervous from before, and the gulls had darted right past his nose!

"Henry!" Laura yelled in panic as the puppy tugged hard at his leash, and it slipped out of her hand.

She dashed after him as he turned
tail and raced back along the path the
way they'd come. He didn't stop until
he came to a tangle of bushes, just at the
edge of the cliff. The stems were thick
and dark with thorns, but he wriggled
underneath.

Laura kneeled down to look at him,
crouching under the bushes. "Oh,

Henry," she whispered.

The puppy peered out at her and whimpered a little. Everything was different and scary, and he didn't understand. First the new house and all those people who kept shouting at him. Then that roaring thing had swooped over his head, so loud it had made his ears hurt. And now the shrieking birds. Everything felt wrong.

"It's all right…." The girl was talking again, so quietly. Her whispers were soothing, and he crept out of the bushes a little, just close enough for her to rub her hand over his head and pet his ears.

He crawled a little farther, plunging his head into her knees and letting her wrap her arms around him. *She smells good*, Henry thought. His racing heart slowed slightly, and he relaxed against her with a shiver.

"Poor Henry," she muttered. "Poor sweetheart. You're safe now."

Chapter Five
A Sneaky Plan

"She really lets you take him for a walk every day?" Jessie asked, wonderingly.

"Every day for the last five days now. I'm so lucky. We went as far as the lighthouse this morning. That's a long walk for him, but he was just fine." Laura smiled down proudly at Henry as he pranced over the sand in front of them. "I didn't think Annie would ever let me take him out again after the first time. He was all sandy, and he had pieces of thistles in his fur when we got back. But she went and got his brush, and we groomed him together. Annie said he seemed to really like me."

"Yes, but why doesn't she want to take him herself?" Jessie asked. "If I had a beautiful dog like that, I wouldn't let other people walk him!"

"I guess she doesn't have time because she's on vacation with her friends. I don't know—I'm just grateful." Laura sighed. "But I'm going to miss him so much when they go. They're only here for one more week. Of course, Mom can't wait for them to leave. Two of the other families have complained that they're too noisy, and she keeps worrying about what's going to go wrong next!"

"Yeah, she was telling my mom about them when they ran into each other in the grocery store. Is your mom okay with you walking him all the time?"

"She said it was fine as long as I tell her where we're going. But she was a little worried when I told her about those seagulls."

Jessie shuddered. "One of them snatched my sandwich last summer when we were having a picnic on the beach. They're huge!"

"Especially when you're the size of Henry," Laura agreed.

They both laughed as Henry stopped and turned around. It was like he understood that they were talking about him.

"Did you tell Annie about the seagulls, too?" Jessie said.

Laura nodded. "I didn't really want to, in case she thought I wasn't taking care of him very well, but I had to explain all those thistles in his fur."

"So what did she say?" Jessie asked.

Laura ruffled Henry's ears. "She said she wasn't very surprised. She should have warned me that he hated loud noises, and it definitely wasn't my fault that he slipped the leash. Oh, look, that's her," Laura said, nudging Jessie. "With the curly hair. I thought they always went to Gull Cove."

"If they were coming here, she could have taken Henry with her. After all, dogs are allowed on this beach," Jessie pointed out.

Laura shrugged—she wasn't sure why Annie hadn't brought him, either. "I guess he wouldn't want to sit still while they all sunbathed...."

Annie was lying on the sand and chatting with one of the other girls from the farmhouse, the one Laura thought was named Molly. Laura had met her when she took Henry back the day before.

Annie sat up as she saw them coming over and shielded her eyes from the sun. "Hi there, Laura! Hi, Henry!"

Henry scampered over to her excitedly, pulling Laura along behind him. He ran across Annie's towel and scratched at her,

69

hoping she'd pet him.

"Ow, ow, claws!" Annie pushed him away gently. She was only wearing a bathing suit, and he was scratching her legs.

Henry sat back, his ears drooping a little, and Laura crouched down to pet him. "It's okay—you can't jump up on people, that's all," she said. But she felt bad for the puppy. He'd just wanted his owner to give him a hug.

Henry wagged his tail slowly as she petted him, and Annie sat up and joined in.

"You're so good with him," Annie told Laura, ruffling Henry's ears.

"Thanks!" Laura smiled at her. "I think he's the nicest dog I've ever met. Jessie thinks he's beautiful, too."

"And really friendly," Jessie added.

Annie smiled. "I know—he's perfect."

"You have to be quiet," Laura whispered. "Mom's out, and I don't think she'll be back for a while, but just in case." She watched happily as Henry sniffed his way around her bedroom. He spent a long time nosing at her sneakers, and Laura made faces at him. "That's disgusting! Yuck!"

Henry sat back and sneezed, looking very surprised at himself. Laura laughed so much she had to hug her arms tight around her ribs to stop them from hurting. His orange eyebrows looked as if they might lift off! But after one last quick sniff at the sneakers, he went on exploring, scratching at Laura's wastebasket to see what was inside. He had his front paws balanced on the edge as he kicked and scrambled his back paws up the side.

"Hey, Henry, that's going to tip over," Laura started to say, hopping up from her bed, but the waste basket had already started falling. Henry collapsed on the floor in a pile of scraps of paper.

"You do look funny, silly dog," Laura told him, stuffing

all the paper back into the wastebasket and scooping him up for a nap. "Come and sit with me on the bed."

It's so hot today—too hot and sticky to be outside in the sun, Laura thought. Especially for a little puppy. So she'd retreated to her room instead. She was sure Annie wouldn't mind her taking Henry up there.

Henry snuggled happily in Laura's lap, and she leaned back against the pile of cushions and soft toys. It was so warm, even with the skylight and windows open. Henry turned himself around a couple of times, yawned hugely, and slumped down again. He still had that puppy knack of falling asleep in seconds, no matter what he was doing.

Laura looked down at Henry lovingly

and stretched out one arm to grab the book from her bedside table. She didn't want to disturb him—he looked so comfy. She'd just read for a little while....

"Laura!"

Laura sat up with a jerk, and Henry started to slide off her lap. As she grabbed him, he snuffled and snorted and woke up, looking surprised.

Laura gaped up at her mom. She'd fallen asleep! They both had! She'd meant to take Henry home long before Mom was due back. She hoped Annie wasn't too worried.

"I'm sorry," she said. "I should have asked...."

Her mom sat down next to her on the bed and tickled Henry under the chin. He wagged his tail happily and stomped across the bed to sniff Mom. Then he slumped down again, still weary, with his chin on her leg.

"Aww," Laura's mom sighed, rubbing his ears. "But I'm still upset with you, Laura," she added quickly. "Yes, you *definitely* should have asked. And I probably would have said no."

"Don't you like him?" Laura said sadly.

"Of course I like him—he's adorable. But he's not yours. That's what worries me. You've been spending so much time with him, and now he's in your bedroom—just like he's your own puppy! He'll be going home soon, and I don't want you to be upset."

Laura's shoulders slumped. "I know he'll go home with Annie. And I already know how much I'll miss him," she admitted in a whisper. "But at least he's happy here with me. I'm not sure Annie is taking care of him very well," she added. "If I didn't walk him, Mom, I don't know if anybody would. They always leave him in the house on his own when they go to the beach. They could easily take him with them."

Mom leaned back against the cushions and looked at Henry. "It's really good that you care about him so much," she said slowly, "but there's not a lot we can do. He belongs to someone else. He's Annie's dog, Laura."

"People who are lucky enough to have

dogs should take better care of them!"
Laura burst out. Her eyes were shining
with tears, but her fists were clenched,
and she looked more angry than upset.

Henry gazed up at her and hunched
his shoulders anxiously. He could hear
the unhappiness in her voice, and he let
out a tiny whimper.

"I'm sorry, Henry. I didn't mean to scare
you." Laura ran her hand gently over
his head, whispering to him soothingly.

Henry padded around in a circle on
the bed, and then scrambled back into
her lap and settled down. He was still
eyeing Laura cautiously, though. He
loved her partly for her quiet, gentle
voice. That high, angry tone was all
wrong—he'd never heard her sound like
that before.

Henry wasn't sure what had happened. He liked the lady sitting next to them, too—she'd petted him and given him attention. But then something she'd said had made Laura's voice turn sharp. Now he looked between Laura and her mom uncertainly.

"He's very quick at picking up on how people feel, isn't he?" Mom said. "He knew right away that you were upset, and he didn't like it."

"I know…. I think he doesn't like how busy and loud the farmhouse is, either," Laura said, glancing up at her worriedly. "When I took him back there yesterday, after our walk with Jessie, a couple of the boys were shouting. They weren't fighting or anything, just yelling because one was upstairs, and one was downstairs, but Henry really flinched. He squashed himself down so he was practically on the floor."

"Well, I guess it isn't for much longer." Mom put her arm around Laura's shoulders. "I'm sorry, Laura, but you know what I mean. If he isn't happy in that noisy house, he'll be better off back at home, won't he?"

"Yes, you're right." Laura's head drooped.

"I've been thinking…." Mom hugged her tighter. "I don't think we could now, not when it's summer and I'm working so much, but maybe later in the year…."

Laura looked at her, confused, and Mom laughed. "What I'm trying to say is—would you like us to get a dog of our own?"

Laura gasped, making Henry blink and look up at her. "Really?"

"Mm-hmm. We could go to the rescue in Linwood. I know they have a lot of dogs looking for homes—maybe not puppies as cute as Henry, but I'm sure they're still beautiful. I could take care of the dog while you're at school. When I'm cleaning the cottages, the dog could come and play in the yard. I'm sure that would be all right."

Laura nodded slowly. "I'd love to have our own dog." She looked down at Henry's silky head, flopped over her lap, and let out a little sigh, although she did her best to hide it from Mom. She should be so happy, and she was, she really was.

But it was so hard to think of loving another dog as much as she loved Henry.

Chapter Six
Trouble at the Farmhouse

"I really love walking him," Laura told Annie as they wandered along the beach together. Laura had stopped over to see if Henry wanted a walk, and Annie had said she'd come, too. "It's been so nice of you to let me," she added.

Henry was darting over the damp sand at the edge of the ocean, making squeaky yapping noises at the waves. "I took him into town with me yesterday, and everybody we met stopped and petted him. He had a fan club outside the candy store," Laura said, giggling as Henry glared fiercely at a pile of seaweed.

"I wish Molly and the others liked him as much you do," said Annie. "She still hasn't forgiven him for chewing up her bag." Then she sighed. "I'm not sure what's going to happen when I go off to college, either. Mom and Dad said I could have a present for finishing my exams, and I'd wanted a puppy for so long…. Mom said she'll take care of him, but she isn't really a dog person. I hope he's going to be okay." She gave her shoulders a little shake and smiled at Laura. "I'm sure he will be—don't look

so worried! Anyway, Laura, why don't you have a dog? You're great with Henry! Is it that your mom is too busy?"

"Actually, she just said we could get a dog from the rescue center! And it's all because of Henry. She said she could see how much I love him, and that maybe I should have a dog of my own." Laura didn't say that she and her mom thought they'd be better dog-owners than Annie, but she was sure it was true. How could Annie have asked for a puppy just a few months before she went away to college?

Annie nodded, looking thoughtful. "Your mom's right," she said. "Oh, I'm sorry, but we'd better head back now, Laura. I said I'd go to the grocery store for chips and things—we're having a party for Zara's birthday tonight."

Henry darted behind the couch with his tail tucked between his legs. He wasn't sure what was going on. He'd been sleeping in his basket in the kitchen when Logan had tripped over it and almost stepped on him. Logan had just groaned and laughed, and then shoved the basket into the utility room.

85

Henry had decided to get out of the way, but somehow the living room was even busier than the kitchen. Everyone seemed to be stomping around, and the music was so loud that it felt like the house was shaking.

He peered around the arm of the couch and whined, looking for Annie. He couldn't see her anywhere. Uncertainly, he scurried along the edge of the room, heading for the open door that led out to the yard. He could smell the fresh air and the sharp, salty tang of the ocean. Maybe Annie was outside. Or maybe he'd find Laura—he was sure her house was somewhere nearby. He could curl up and snuggle with her on her bed again. That would be a much better place to sleep.

Henry nosed his way out into the dark yard....

"Laura? Are you awake, sweetheart?"

Laura sat up in bed. She was half awake. She'd been dreaming, and everything still felt strange and dreamlike now. The thudding sound of the music from her dream was still there. She shook her head, trying to shake it away, but it didn't help.

Laura blinked and rubbed her eyes, realizing at last that the music was real. And loud!

"What's going on?"

"The people from the farmhouse, again," Mom sighed. "I'm going to have to tell them to turn the music off. It's one o'clock in the morning! I thought I'd better wake you up and tell you. I'll be back soon, though, okay?"

Laura nodded and peered out her window. The farmhouse was all lit up, and she could see the shadows of people dancing against the curtains. The music was so loud that her window seemed to be shaking.

"Henry!" Laura gasped, suddenly imagining the little dog shut in the house with all that noise. He must be terrified. She leaped out of bed, shoving her feet into her slippers and grabbing a sweatshirt. Then she hurried down the stairs. Mom hadn't locked the front door, so Laura could just slip out behind her.

"What are you doing?" her mom asked, jumping as Laura touched her sleeve. "You scared me, Laura. I didn't even hear you coming up behind me." She rolled her eyes. "I guess that isn't a surprise, is it?"

"I just remembered about Henry," Laura explained. "I'm worried about him, Mom."

"Oh, dear, I hadn't thought of that. Poor little dog!" Mom knocked on the door, and Laura stood next to her, huddled into her sweatshirt. She hoped that Annie and her friends weren't going to be annoyed about being asked to turn off the music.

The yard looked so different in the dark, full of odd shadows and strange shapes. Laura caught her breath, her heart suddenly thumping as one of the shadows moved—and came slinking toward them. She grabbed her mom's arm with a squeak.

"What is it? Oh, honestly, are they never going to answer this door?"

"Mom, there's something...." The shadow settled into a little brown and white shape, padding across the yard. "Oh! Oh, Henry, it's you!" Laura gave a shaky laugh. For about half a second, she really had wondered if it was a ghost!

"Henry?" Mom turned around to look. "He's out here on his own?" Shaking her head angrily, she banged on the door again.

Laura scooped Henry up in her arms, hugging him tightly. He licked her cheek and snuggled his head under her chin.

"Did you slip out? Was it too noisy for you, too? Poor puppy! I wish I could just take you back to the cottage with me. I'd take care of you."

She perched on the bench outside the farmhouse, loving the feel of the puppy in her arms, squirmy and soft. "I bet they haven't even noticed you're gone," she whispered in Henry's fluffy ear. Then she sat up straighter, suddenly getting an idea. "Mom…. Couldn't we just take Henry back home with us for the rest of the night? He's scared

91

of the noise."

Mom shook her head sadly. "I wish we could, Laura. But don't worry—I'm going to make them turn the music down. Oh, at last!"

Someone had finally opened the door. One of the boys was standing there, peering out as though he was surprised to see Laura's mom. It was Logan, the one she'd seen taking Henry out that first day, Laura realized.

"Yes?" he said sullenly.

"Can you please turn that music off! Do you know what time it is?"

Laura's mom sounded really annoyed.

If it had been me, Laura thought, *I would have done as I was told right away.* That was the kind of voice

Mom used when she was sending
Laura to her room. But Logan didn't
seem to care. He just kept saying that
it wasn't all that late. Laura could tell
that her mom was getting angrier by
the second, and she could feel Henry
tensing up in her arms.

"Come on," she muttered. "I'll have to take you back in a minute, but not until everything is quiet again. It isn't fair." She hurried around the corner of the farmhouse, where the angry voices weren't so clear, and stood there petting Henry and whispering to him.

"Oh!" The music went off, and the sudden silence was eerie. It sounded almost louder than the music had, and the night seemed darker all at once. Laura felt Henry wriggle in her arms. "I know, I guess we should go back. I'll bet Mom told them about you, too, by now." Reluctantly, Laura padded around the corner of the house.

"There you are!" Her mom sounded relieved.

"I'm sorry—Henry was scared."

Laura came up to the door and looked at Logan. Several other people were behind him now, and Laura wished she'd stayed to support her mom. It must have been really hard having to tell them all what to do. None of them looked very happy.

Laura peered around Mom's shoulder. Annie wasn't there, but she could see Annie's friend Molly.

Laura was just about to ask where Annie was, so she could give Henry back, when Molly stepped forward. "How did he get out here?" she asked. "I bet someone left that gate open again."

"We found him in the yard. He doesn't like loud noises and shouting…," Laura whispered, holding him out to Molly.

Molly grabbed him, but Henry wriggled and twisted, and Molly squealed and let go. He landed heavily on the floor with a yelp. Then he crept back to Laura, whining and pressing himself miserably against her legs.

Laura was gentle and friendly, and her house was quiet. She played with him, and took him for walks, and didn't yank his leash to hurry him up. Even when he was scared, like tonight, Laura always protected him. He slunk around behind Laura's fluffy slippers and barked at the other girl. He barked as loudly as he could, but it came out as a shrill, frightened noise.

"Oh, stop it, you silly dog. Come here," Molly said, leaning down to grab him again.

Henry snapped his teeth at her angrily, just grazing the back of her hand. He didn't really mean to bite, but everything was just so scary.

"Hey!" Molly snatched her hand away with a gasp. "Ow! Bad dog!"

Henry heard Laura protest, but Molly picked him up again and marched into the house. Henry peered over her arm, scratching and whining and looking for Laura. He could still see her, leaning against her mom and crying. He clawed at the girl's sleeve, trying to wriggle free, but this time, he couldn't get away.

"Naughty dog! No biting!" Molly said, carrying him into the utility room and dropping him onto the tiles. "Just stay there!"

She slammed the door, and Henry crouched in front of it, shaking all over. He was all alone and so scared.

Whimpering, he turned around and slunk across the floor to his basket. He climbed in, pressing his head against the soft side and burrowing half under the crumpled blanket. He wanted to hide from everything.

Chapter Seven
Leaving Early

"Are they really going to go home? Even though they're supposed to stay almost another week?" Laura stared at her mom. She felt like crying.

"They have to," Mom said with a sigh. "I spoke to Jenny from the rental agency this morning, after I'd already had three different families complaining to me about the noise. She says she'll call them and explain that they have to leave."

"Today?" Laura asked, her voice very small.

"I think so. I'm sorry, sweetheart." Mom hugged her. "But I bet Henry will be happy to go home. He hasn't liked being in a house full of people."

"We don't know what his home is like," Laura muttered into her mom's sleeve. "Maybe that's full of people, too. Annie might have a lot of brothers and sisters." She couldn't help feeling sad. She felt too miserable to look on the bright side. Her mom just hugged her tighter. She could tell how upset Laura was.

"Do you think I'll be able to say good-bye to him?" Laura said, her voice still

muffled, so that
her mom had to
tilt her head to
listen.

"I hope so. I'll
have to go over
to pick up the keys
and make sure they've
left the house nice and clean. You can
come with me, if you'd like. Although
no one is going to be in a very good
mood," she warned.

Laura looked up and nodded, biting
her lip. She didn't really want to listen to
another argument like the night before,
but she couldn't miss the chance to say
good-bye to Henry.

"I'm glad you won't have everybody
complaining to you anymore," she said,

resting her head against her mom's shoulder.

"Me, too. And, Laura, I really did mean it about us getting a dog. You've been so good at helping with Henry. Very responsible. Try to think of the positive side of things, okay?"

Laura nodded. She was trying. But all she could think of was Henry last night, whimpering as Molly carried him away.

Henry was sitting underneath the coffee table. He didn't really want to be there, but he didn't know where else to go. He'd been curled up on Annie's lap, enjoying being cuddled and petted, when the sharp sound of the doorbell had made him jump. And it had made everyone start shouting again. Annie had gotten up, leaving him on the couch, but there was just too much noise to stay there. So he'd clambered down into the small, safe space under the table.

Maybe he should go and sit in his basket…. If he went to sleep for a while, maybe everything would quiet down again. Henry poked his nose out from under the table and then pulled it back quickly as a suitcase on wheels went rattling by. But then he shook himself briskly and went trotting out after the case. He wasn't going to sleep. He would go and find Laura instead. They could go for a walk. Or even just snuggle up together, the way they had the other day.

Both times when he'd gotten out of

the house before, he'd slipped out of the side gate in the yard, so he went that way again, keeping close to the walls and skittering past the piles of bags and beach stuff. Whenever he heard people come hurrying past, Henry froze. But no one seemed to notice him anyway. The back door that led into the little yard was open, like it had been the night before, and Henry slipped out. His feathery tail started to wag delightedly back and forth. He would see Laura soon!

But the gate onto the path was closed. Henry sat in front of it, confused, his tail sweeping from side to side on the dusty path. He had only ever seen it open. This wasn't right. After a minute or so, it was clear that the gate wasn't going to move. He got up and sniffed at it, and then stood up on his hind paws and scratched away, but all it did was creak a little and rattle. It stayed firmly shut.

Henry gave the gate one last hopeful look. Then he sniffed at the tall plants growing beside the fence and peered between the slats. There was the path. That was the way Laura had always taken him. He was sure that that path would take him back to her.

Henry crept along the base of the fence, pushing his way through the thick stems and scratching half-heartedly at the wooden posts here and there. But the fence was solid, and the wooden slats were too close together even for a little dog to squeeze through. Henry slumped down under a clump of poppies, feeling helpless. His coat was tangled, full of grass seeds and twigs. He was hot and upset—and he was still stuck. He sank his chin down on his paws and gazed miserably at the ground. Then his nose twitched thoughtfully.

Right in front of him, there was a small dip under the fence. It had started as nothing more than a puddle of rain dripping down from a bush, but the water had smoothed the earth away, and now there was a definite hollow. Almost big enough for a little dog to squirm through....

Henry sprang up with an excited whine and began to scrape and scratch with his soft puppy claws at the dry earth. It only took a few minutes to widen the hole and dig it a little deeper, and then deeper still ... until it was just big enough for him to force his head under. He squeezed and wriggled until he was outside on the path.

Henry looked around triumphantly and shook the dusty earth out of his fur. Then he set off, his head held high, to find Laura.

Laura stood next to her mom—as close as she could. Laura wanted Mom to know that she was right there beside her. Logan was telling Mom that it was completely unfair that they were being forced to leave. Laura thought it wasn't fair that her mom just had to stand there and listen to people shouting at her again.

"I can see that you're upset, but the best thing to do is to send an e-mail to the rental agency," Mom said patiently.

Laura peered around Mom, trying to see into the other rooms. She wasn't sure where Henry was. She could see his basket in the utility room, but he wasn't in it. Maybe he was hiding somewhere, because of all the angry voices.

"I just need to check around the house to make sure that everything's okay," Mom explained. "It looks like you're mostly packed up. Are you bringing the cars around to the front? You can put them in the yard for loading up, if you'd like."

Laura trailed after Mom around the upstairs rooms. The group was really going, any minute now. If she didn't find Henry soon, she wouldn't be able to say good-bye to him at all. *Maybe Annie had taken him for one last walk,* she thought sadly.

But then she saw Annie packing up stuff from one of the bathrooms. So that 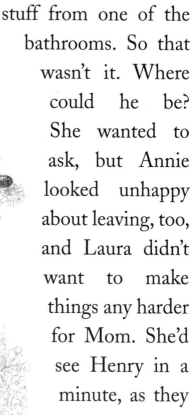 wasn't it. Where could he be? She wanted to ask, but Annie looked unhappy about leaving, too, and Laura didn't want to make things any harder for Mom. She'd see Henry in a minute, as they were putting him in the car. Even if it was just for one last quick snuggle.

Chapter Eight
Where's Henry?

Henry peered around the corner of the farmhouse, eyeing the commotion in the yard. He wanted to see if he could find Laura, but a car had driven up, and then another one, both braking sharply and sending up a spray of gravel and dust.

A car door slammed, and he flinched. Maybe he wouldn't go this way. Henry looked around nervously. Maybe Laura was at the beach. But he wasn't sure if he wanted to go farther down the clifftop path by himself. Instead, he padded a little way across the gravel and crept in between two large pots of flowers. He'd sit here and watch for Laura.

And then, there she was! Coming out of the farmhouse— she had been there the entire time!

Henry yelped and poked his nose out from between the flowerpots. But then a car door slammed again, and there were

113

people everywhere, flinging bags into the cars and shouting to each other. He didn't dare go past them. Henry wriggled back, deeper into the little damp space between the pots. The trailing leaves hid him, and he felt safe, but he couldn't reach Laura....

Laura stood with her mom by the front door of the farmhouse, looking at the two cars. Neither of them had space for a travel crate for a dog, she noticed. She couldn't even see any room for Henry to sit. If they put him in the back with all those bags, one of them could easily topple over and squash him.

"Mom," she said, tugging at her

mom's sleeve. "I still haven't seen Henry. He wasn't in the house."

Her mom glanced down at her. "He wasn't? Actually, I don't think I saw him, either...."

Just then, Annie came hurrying out the front door, her face pale under her tan. "Has anyone seen Henry?" she asked. "I still can't find him, and I've been looking everywhere!"

"I thought he was shut in the utility room," Logan called back. "You said you wanted to keep him out of the way while we were packing."

"Yes, I know. But he isn't there now," Annie said. "The front door is wide open. And so is the back one."

Laura glanced worriedly at her mom. Maybe Henry had gone down to the beach on his own. He could be anywhere.

"Yeah, but the gate in the backyard is shut, isn't it?" Molly straightened up, frowning. She'd been shoving bags into one of the cars, and now she pushed her hair out of her eyes, looking grumpy and hot. "He escaped that way the other times, so we've all been really careful about keeping it closed today."

"Then where is he?" Annie wailed. "He's not in the house. I've checked everywhere, under all the beds. I even went through all the cupboards. He must have gotten out."

Logan closed the trunk of the car with a thump. It barely closed, with the car so packed.

"Not even sure we can fit him in the

car," he called to Annie. "Maybe you should just leave him here."

Laura stared at him in horror. She thought he must be joking—he had to be! But he wasn't smiling.

She clenched her fists, suddenly furious. How dare he?

"You can't just leave Henry behind. It's because of people like you that there are rescue centers full of abandoned dogs!" Laura yelled at him. "How can you say that? You don't even know where he is! He could be lost on the cliff, or down on the beach." Then she drew back against her mom, feeling her cheeks redden.

Logan shrugged, but he looked embarrassed, too. "I didn't actually mean we'd leave him…," he muttered.

"Of course I'm not leaving him!" Annie gulped. It seemed as though she was about to cry. "Laura, do you really think he could have gone all the way down to the beach?"

Laura nodded. "He loves it there."

"Well, don't be too long." Logan

folded his arms, leaning against the car.

"I'll come and help look." Laura started to follow Annie, and then glanced back at her mom to check that it was okay.

"Yes, you'd better," her mom said. "I'll come, too, once I have the keys."

Laura followed Annie along the front of the house to the corner where the path started. She was trying to think of all the places Henry might be. Where had he really liked to be when they'd been out on walks? Maybe he was digging around in one of those smelly seaweed piles on the beach again.

Then something made her glance sideways, down at the flowerpots. Maybe it was a tiny whimper, or maybe a scuffling of puppy claws.

He was there—gazing out at her. Laura could see his tail, wagging just a little, as though he wasn't quite sure whether to be happy. He didn't want to come out, she guessed. Too much shouting and banging.

Laura stopped. She'd have to tell

Annie, of course. Only … if she didn't, maybe they would go without him, like Logan had said. Maybe they'd leave Henry, and she could keep him…. Laura dug her fingernails into her palms, hesitating.

No—she had to say something. Even though she really, really didn't want to.

Laura took a deep breath and called after Annie, who was just disappearing around the corner of the house. "He's here!"

"Henry!" Annie came dashing over, her footsteps crunching on the gravel. But the puppy edged backward, farther into the space between the pots.

"I think he's scared," Laura said sadly. She glanced around and saw that Mom had hurried up next to her.

She looked sad, too.

"Come on, Henry," Annie called.

"Can't you just grab him?" Logan yelled.

Annie turned around to glare at him. "Be quiet, Logan! He doesn't like people shouting—you're making it worse. Come on, Henry...."

Laura kneeled down in front of the pots and looked in at the puppy. "Henry," she whispered. "It's okay. Come on out."

Henry eyed her and then glanced at Annie. Very slowly, he started to creep toward them, paw by paw, as though he wasn't sure if he was doing the right thing. He then made a sudden little rush and jumped at Laura, scrambling onto her lap. He was shivering, and Laura wrapped her arms around him.

She stood up slowly and rubbed her cheek against his soft fur one last time. Then, reluctantly, she held him out to Annie.

Annie looked at her for a moment. At last she shook her head. "No," she said quietly. "No. I think you'd better keep him. You'll take care of him a lot better than I have."

"W-what?" Laura stammered. She'd wished and wished for Annie to say exactly that. Now she thought she might have imagined it.

"Keep him. He can be yours, if you'd like."

"Hang on…." Laura's mom shook her head. "That's really nice of you, but we can't just take him!"

"Oh, Mom!" Laura gasped, her eyes filling with tears. "Please…." She'd been so happy, just for a second.

But Annie smiled—a stiff, unhappy smile. "I shouldn't ever have asked for him. It was really selfish of me. He'll be much happier with you." She sighed and put out her hand to rub Henry's soft ears. "I'll miss you," she told him.

"Well…." Laura's mom frowned. "I guess, if you're sure."

"So I can keep him?" Laura asked, in a whisper.

Mom nodded. "Yes!"

Annie turned away quickly and grabbed Henry's basket and bowls and food out of the car. She pushed them into Mom's arms and then dived into the front seat as though she wanted to get away as quickly as possible.

Laura stood watching as the cars backed slowly out of the yard. Henry was still in her arms—they were going, really going, and leaving Henry behind with her. She stared down at him anxiously. Would he be upset, seeing Annie leave? But he looked very happy snuggled up against her T-shirt.

"I have a dog!" she said to Mom, only half believing it. Was this all just some kind of dream?

"You do!" Mom agreed, her eyes wide. "Oh my goodness! We have a dog...."

She glanced at the basket and bowls and bag of food she was holding and shook her head slightly. "I guess we'd better go and put these inside."

As Laura followed her mom back into the house, Henry licked her ear, making her giggle. She couldn't be dreaming, if her ear was all wet.... She stood in the hall with Henry, kicking off her flip-flops, and watched Mom hang the puppy's red leash on one of the coat hooks.

"It looks perfect," Laura whispered in Henry's ear. "It looks just like you belong!"